Note to parents, carers and teachers

Read it yourself is a series of modern stories, favourite characters and traditional tales written in a simple way for children who are learning to read. The books can be read independently or as part of a guided reading session.

Each book is carefully structured to include many high-frequency words vital for first reading. The sentences on each page are supported closely by pictures to help with understanding, and to offer lively details to talk about.

The books are graded into four levels that progressively introduce wider vocabulary and longer stories as a reader's ability and confidence grows.

Ideas for use

- Ask how your child would like to approach reading at this stage. Would he prefer to hear you read the story first, or would he like to read the story to you and see how he gets on?

- Help him to sound out any words he does not know.

- Developing readers can be concentrating so hard on the words that they sometimes don't fully grasp the meaning of what they're reading. Answering the puzzle questions at the back of the book will help with understanding.

For more information and advice on Read it yourself and book banding, visit **www.ladybird.com/readityourself**

Book
Band
9

Level 3 is ideal for children who are developing reading confidence and stamina, and who are eager to read longer stories with a wider vocabulary.

Special features:

Wider vocabulary, reinforced through repetition

Detailed pictures for added interest and discussion

As time went by, Baloo the bear showed Mowgli how to make jungle calls.

Bagheera the panther heard about Mowgli and came to see him.

10

11

Longer sentences

Simple story structure

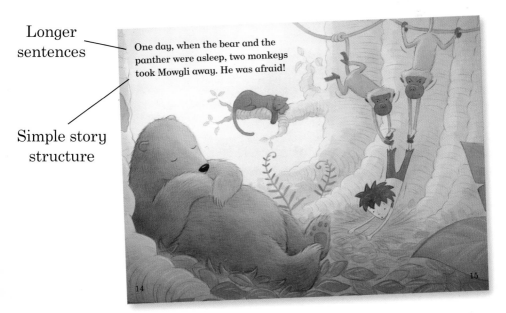

One day, when the bear and the panther were asleep, two monkeys took Mowgli away. He was afraid!

14

15

Educational Consultant: Geraldine Taylor
Book Banding Consultant: Kate Ruttle

A catalogue record for this book is available from the British Library

Published by Ladybird Books Ltd
80 Strand, London, WC2R 0RL
A Penguin Company

006

ISBN: 978-0-72328-079-8

Printed in China

The Jungle Book

Written by Jillian Powell
Illustrated by Gavin Scott

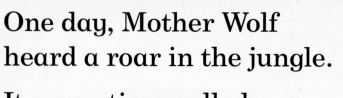

One day, Mother Wolf
heard a roar in the jungle.

It was a tiger called
Shere Khan. He had found a
man-cub and was chasing him.

"We will keep that man-cub safe,"
Mother Wolf told Father Wolf.
"We will call him Mowgli."

Shere Khan was angry.
He wanted to eat the man-cub.

"I'll be back for him," he roared.

As time went by, Baloo the bear showed Mowgli how to make jungle calls.

Bagheera the panther heard about Mowgli and came to see him.

Mowgli wanted to play
with the monkeys.

But Baloo and Bagheera said,
"You can't trust monkeys. It's not
safe to play with them."

One day, when the bear and the panther were asleep, two monkeys took Mowgli away. He was afraid!

Mowgli looked up and saw Chil, the kite. He made a kite call to him and Chil came over.

"Get Baloo and Bagheera to help me!" Mowgli said.

Chil found Baloo and Bagheera, and told them that the monkeys had got Mowgli.

Bagheera said, "Kaa the python will help us. The monkeys are afraid of him."

The monkeys kept Mowgli in a snake house. He made a snake call to stop the snakes biting him.

Then he saw Bagheera the panther! The monkeys jumped on Bagheera and bit him.
"Go in the water!" Mowgli called. "That will stop them."

When Baloo came to help, the monkeys jumped on him, too!

Just then, they heard Kaa the python hiss and the monkeys ran away!

Baloo helped Mowgli get
out of the snake house.
Mowgli was safe with
Baloo and Bagheera again.

27

Some time went by. One day
Bagheera the panther said,
"The wolves want a new leader
and they will not want a man-cub
with them. You are not one
of them, you are not a wolf."

"You are not safe here," said Bagheera. "Go and live in the village."

"One day I will come back with the skin of Shere Khan!" Mowgli said. "Then the wolves will see what I can do!"

Mowgli went to the village
and all the people came
out to see him. A woman
called Messua said she
was Mowgli's mother.
She looked after him.

33

In the village, Mowgli lived with the people and looked after the buffalo herd.

One day when Mowgli was with the buffalo, two wolves came to see him. One of the wolves was called Grey Brother.

"Shere Khan is back. He wants to eat you," said Grey Brother.

"Take half the buffalo herd this way and half that way," said Mowgli.

When the tiger came, Mowgli called the herd.

The buffalo ran right over Shere Khan!

Mowgli came back with the tiger skin.

The village people said, "We want that skin to sell it."

Mowgli said it was his. The people were very angry.

"You have to go," Messua said. "You are not safe here."

So Mowgli went back to the jungle.

When the wolves saw Shere Khan's skin, they said, "You can be our new leader!"

But Mowgli said, "No, you did not want me with you, so I will live alone."

"Trust me," said Grey Brother. "Live with me."

Mowgli did trust Grey Brother, so he went to live with him in the jungle.

And Baloo and Bagheera were happy that he was safe.

How much do you remember about the story of The Jungle Book? Answer these questions and find out!

- Who is chasing Mowgli in the jungle?

- Who teaches Mowgli to make jungle calls?

- Where do the monkeys take Mowgli?

- Which animals run over Shere Khan?

- Who does Mowgli go to live with at the end?

Look at the different story sentences and match them to the characters who said them.

"We will call him Mowgli."

"I'll be back for him."

"You are not safe here. Go and live in the village."

"One day I will come back with the skin of Shere Khan!"

Read it yourself with Ladybird

Tick the books you've read!

For more confident readers who can read simple stories with help.

Level **3**

☐ ☐ ☐ ☐ ☐ ☐

☐ ☐ ☐ ☐ ☐ ☐ ☐ ☐

Longer stories for more independent, fluent readers.

Level **4**

☐ ☐ ☐ ☐ ☐ ☐

☐ ☐ ☐ ☐ ☐ ☐ ☐ ☐